Thank You, Body
A GOODNIGHT BOOK

By Sharon Khen

Illustrated by Joseph Stellato

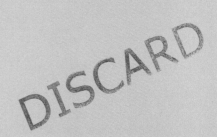

ISBN: 0615782019
ISBN-13: 9780615782010

This book was inspired by my journey to good health after
battling cancer and its remaining complications.

I would like to dedicate this book to my dear family and friends:
My husband, Oded, the love of my life
My beloved children—Golan, Yahav, and Edan—
my everyday inspiration and true blessings
All my loved ones who were and still are with me
every step of the way.

You all are the embodiment of unconditional love,
and I am grateful to have you in my life.

Dear Parents,

As a mother of three and an experienced drama-and-play therapist and psychotherapist, working with children for over ten years, I have had the privilege of witnessing their fascinating inner world. As parents, we are very familiar with our children's everyday rituals. They ask for a specific book to be read to them over and over again or for the exact number of very particular hugs and kisses when saying good-bye before we leave them at preschool in the morning or for the same special lullaby at bedtime. These are not just habits; they are special rituals in our children's routines, and they serve an important role in their psychological well-being.

Children are constantly processing the dynamic world around them and positioning themselves accordingly. This process can be overwhelming and often scary, and their rituals create a temporary sense of control over their world—they are familiar, contain no surprises, and are predictable. They help children feel less anxious, more secure, and confident.

This book is a bedtime soothing ritual wherein a child thanks each part of their body and acknowledges it for letting them be the special child they are. The book also contributes to a child's positive body image and self-esteem, and it offers an opportunity for special parent-child quality time because of its interactive nature. Just lie down in bed next to your child and read while pointing out and celebrating each body part. You'll see the calming effect it has as you read. In the end, have your child stretch their whole body (as in the book) and then slowly release their energy, transitioning into a peaceful feeling, just in time for a good night's sleep. Enjoy!

To our children's rituals!
Sharon Khen

As I lie down and lower the light,

I take a deep breath to welcome the night.

I feel how my body rests on the bed

And thank each part, from my toes to my head.

Thank you, dear toes and sweet little feet;

Thank you for tapping to each little beat.

Thank you for balancing all of my weight.

Goodnight, my dear feet—you both are so great!

Thank you, dear legs, for being so strong.

Thank you for walking and dancing along.

Thank you for running and standing quite still.

Thank you for moving when that is my will.

Now it is time for you both to rest;

Goodnight, my dear legs—you two are the best!

Thank you, dear tummy, for letting me know

When I am hungry and when I must go...

Thank you for welcoming all that I eat,

Like bread and cheese and cookies and meat.

Thanks for the butterflies when I'm so excited;

Thank you, dear tummy—you make me delighted!

Now it is time for you to count sheep,

And I wish you, dear tummy, a long, good night's sleep.

Thank you, dear chest and my strong lungs, too,

For doing the important job that you do.

Thank you for being as strong as a whale;

Thank you for letting me inhale and exhale.

Thank you for working nonstop and so hard;

Thank you for always being on guard—

Watching me breathe in all situations.

Thank you for never taking vacations.

So, dear chest, nighty night, night nighty;

Thank you, dear lungs—you're so very mighty!

Thank you, dear heart, for letting me feel

Each and every feeling for real.

Thank you for having so much room,

Letting me to go from joy to gloom.

Thanks for when I feel happy and glad;

Thanks for when I feel angry and mad.

Thanks for when I feel scared and you shake;

Thanks for when I feel sad and you ache.

Thank you for all of those feelings above.

Thank you the most for the feeling of love.

Thanks for reflecting it all on my face.

Thanks for teaching me how to embrace

All of these wonderful feelings inside;

Thank you, for now I am feeling such pride.

Thank you, dear heart—you're my favorite part!

Thank you, strong shoulders, for carrying much:

My neck, my arms, my worries, and such.

Thank you for holding it all together,

Making it look as light as a feather.

Thank you, dear shoulders, for all your support.

Goodnight to you—you're such a good sport!

Thank you, dear arms, I love when you dare

To get close to a loved one and hug like a bear.

Please, great arms, for I need to share—

I love to hug…don't make it too rare.

Thank you so much, my cuddly arms,

For you have become my lucky charms.

Now it is time for the moon to glow,

So goodnight, dear arms—I thank you so!

Thank you, dear hands, both the left and the right,

For letting me touch, and to draw, and to write.

Thank you for when you clap and you play;

Thank you for what you create out of clay.

Thank you for building…and for cleaning up;

Thank you for holding my fork and my cup.

Thank you for waving hello and good-bye;

Thank you for how you button and tie.

Thank you for giving and receiving, too—

Those, the most gracious things that you do.

Thank you for whether you're dirty or tidy;

Thank you for always being almighty.

It's truly amazing how much you can do.

Goodnight, dear hands—I now salute you!

Thank you, dear neck, for being so bendy;

With a scarf or a tie, you look very trendy.

Thank you so much for when you are able

To hold yourself tight, be strong and be stable,

For my head does depend upon you all alone—

You, my dear neck, are its beautiful throne.

Now it is time to loosen you up;

Goodnight, my dear neck—you get two thumbs up!

Thank you, dear head, for allowing the space

For all of the beautiful parts of my face.

I'll thank them all right here and now,

And for each of them I'll take a bow:

My mouth for eating…and speaking my mind,

My nose for smelling scents of all kind,

My ears for hearing and noting each sound,

My eyes for seeing and looking around.

For it's magical and truly profound,

How they all sense the world around.

Thank you, dear face, for it is impressive

How charming you are, and so very expressive.

Goodnight to you and to each little part;

Tomorrow we face an exciting new start.

Thank you, dear head, and I thank you sincerely

For creating my thoughts and for thinking them clearly.

Thank you for having no limits or border;

Thank you for putting my world all in order.

Thank you for focusing and learning all day;

Thank you for dreaming and drifting away.

Thanks for creating a tale or a song;

Thanks for showing me a right from a wrong.

Thanks for being my teacher and guide;

Thanks for whenever I choose and decide:

On what I like and when I disagree,

For all of these things are what make me, me.

'Cause thoughts, even when silly or wild,

Make me such a special child.

So very special—one of a kind,

Thanks to you—to my dear mind.

Now it's time to rest in bed;

Goodnight to you, my precious head.

Goodnight, dear body, I thank you deeply.

Now it's time to relax completely.

To stretch all my parts, and then let them drop,

To close my eyes slowly, and let the world stop.

"Thank you forever," I whisper to you;

I promise I'll take good care of you, too.

Now I feel very peaceful and free—

You truly are a gift to me.

CPSIA information can be obtained
at www.ICGtesting.com
Printed in the USA
LVIC06n1600290414
383724LV00022B/230